W9-AYE-565

NEW ROCHELLE PUBLIC LIBRARY

Willie's
Not the Hugging Kind

Willie's
Not the Hugging Kind

by Joyce Durham Barrett

illustrated by Pat Cummings

Harper & Row, Publishers

Willie's Not the Hugging Kind
Text copyright © 1989 by Joyce Durham Barrett
Illustrations copyright © 1989 by Pat Cummings
All rights reserved. No part of this book may be
used or reproduced in any manner whatsoever without
written permission except in the case of brief quotations
embodied in critical articles and reviews. Printed in
the United States of America. For information address
Harper & Row Junior Books, 10 East 53rd Street,
New York, N.Y. 10022.
Typography by Pat Tobin
10 9 8 7 6 5 4 3 2 1
First Edition

Library of Congress Cataloging-in-Publication Data
Barrett, Joyce Durham.
  Willie's not the hugging kind / written by Joyce Durham Barrett :
illustrated by Pat Cummings.
      p.   cm.
  Summary: Willie's best friend Jo-Jo thinks hugging is silly,
so Willie stops hugging everybody but he soon misses giving
and getting hugs from his family.
  ISBN 0-06-020416-8 : $. — ISBN 0-06-020417-6 (lib. bdg.) : $
  [1. Hugging—Fiction.   2. Friendship—Fiction.   3. Self-
confidence—Fiction.]   I. Cummings, Pat, ill.   II. Title.
PZ7.B275195Wi 1989   89-1868
[E]—dc19   CIP
                                                            AC

To Lydia, with appreciation to Michael
—JDB

For my uncle, Robert Taylor
—PC

Willie wanted someone to hug. That's what he wanted more than anything.

But no one hugged Willie. Not anymore.

Not even his daddy when he dropped Willie and his friend Jo-Jo off at school. Now, he just patted Willie on the head and said, "See you around, Son."

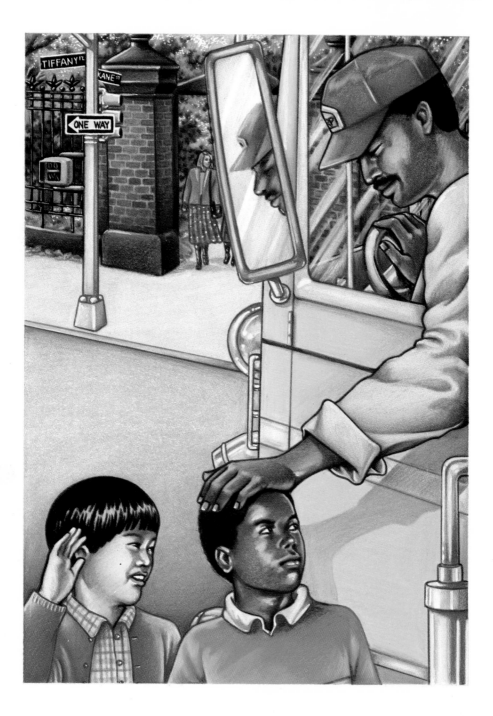

Willie didn't like to be patted on the head. It made him feel like a little dog. Besides, hugging felt much nicer, no matter what Jo-Jo said.

Every day Jo-Jo rode to school in the linen truck with Willie and his daddy. And when Willie used to hug his daddy good-bye, Jo-Jo would turn his head and laugh. "What did you do that for? Man, that's silly," Jo-Jo would say once they had crawled out of the truck.

So Willie stopped hugging his daddy. He never hugged his mama or his sister anymore either. And when they tried to hug Willie, he turned away. But Willie wanted someone to hug. That's what he wanted more than anything.

At school he watched as Miss Mary put her arms around some boy or girl. It didn't look silly. Except when she tried to hug Jo-Jo. Jo-Jo made a big commotion that made everyone laugh. He wriggled and squirmed, and shrieked, "Help! Help! I'm being mugged! Help!"

At night Willie watched his sister pull her teddy bear to her and hug it. She looked so safe and happy lying there with her arms around the bear.

"Why do you hug that old thing?" Willie said. "That's silly."

Rose frowned at Willie. "Who says?" she demanded.

"Jo-Jo says, that's who says," Willie boasted.

"Well, if you ask me, I think Jo-Jo's silly," said Rose. "Besides," she said, squeezing the bear to her, "Homer's nice."

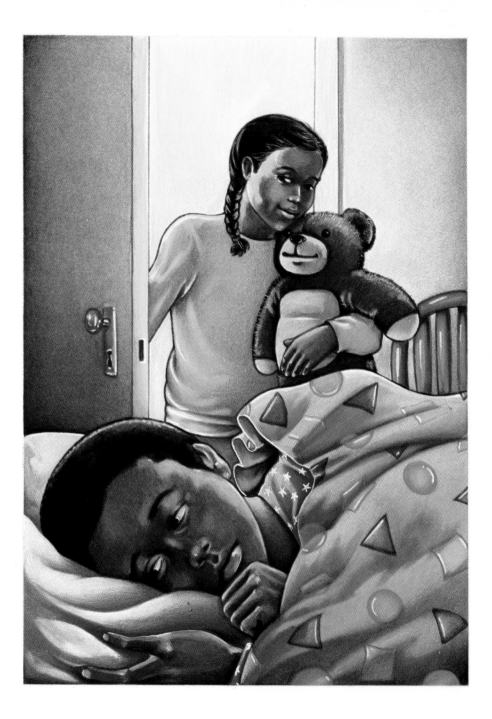

But the next night Willie pinched his nose and said, "What a smelly old bear! I wouldn't hug that old thing for a hundred dollars. Not even for a million dollars. That's silly."

Rose pulled Homer in closer to her. "Willie," she said, "you're just not the hugging kind, then...if that's how you feel."

Willie flipped over in bed without even saying, "Good night, sleep tight, God keep you alright." And his mind went around and around on what his sister had said. The words tick-tocked back and forth with the clock sitting on the table by his bed:

NOT-the hugging kind,
NOT-the hugging kind,
NOT-the hugging kind,
if-THAT'S-how-you-feel.

But that was not how Willie felt. More than anything, Willie wanted to be the hugging kind.

Willie watched each morning as his daddy hugged first his mama and then Rose. He remembered how safe and happy he always felt with his daddy's strong arms around him.

He remembered how good it felt to put his arms around his mama. She smelled a little like lemon and a little like the lilac powder in the bathroom. She felt big and a little lumpy. She also felt soft and safe and warm.

One morning Willie went into the kitchen and everyone was hugging everyone else. But no one hugged Willie. They didn't even see him. Willie waited, hoping someone would put their arms around him. If they did, maybe he wouldn't slip away.

But no one tried. Rose just said, when she saw Willie watching, "You know that Willie says he isn't the hugging kind now. He says it's all too, too silly."

"I did not!" said Willie, bristling. "Jo-Jo said that!"

"Oh, but you said it too, Little Brother," Rose said, laughing and tousling his hair.

19

Willie grabbed his lunch and his books, and ran out the door to meet Jo-Jo. "Let's get out of here!" Willie shrieked, breaking into a run. "They're mugging everybody in there!"

That afternoon Jo-Jo's mother picked him up after school, so Willie walked home alone.

He walked through the park and saw a young couple standing on the footbridge with their arms around each other.

He walked down Myrtle Street and saw a woman and a man rushing down the steps from their porch to greet some visitors with hugs all around.

It seemed so long since Willie had had a hug.

He walked into the long, low branches of a willow tree and wrapped his arms around it. A blue jay flew down from a purple plum tree, and Willie reached out to its fluttering wings. He walked up to a stop sign and hugged it.

He hugged his bike in the front yard. He hugged the door to his house when he opened it. And he rushed inside to hug his mama. But she was too busy running the vacuum over the floors. Willie was kind of glad. After all, he felt a little silly.

That night, after Willie had had his bath, he took the old bath towel and draped it across the head of his bed.

"What's that for?" Rose asked, hugging Homer to her.

"Nothing," said Willie.

The next night Willie put the old bath towel on the bed again. And the next night, and the next. Each night, when he was sure that Rose was not watching, he slipped the old towel down from the headboard and he hugged it. But it didn't feel soft and safe and warm.

Willie wanted to hug someONE, not someTHING.

In the morning Willie's mama was in the kitchen making biscuits. He watched Rose brush up to her and put her arms around her.

When the biscuits were finished and browning in the oven, Willie went up and put his arms around his mama too. Or almost around her. There was a little more to her than he remembered. She felt much nicer than an old towel. And, even better, she hugged back.

"What's all this, Willie," she said, "hugging around here on me so early in the morning?"

"Yeah, Willie," said Rose. "I thought all that hugging was too, too silly."

Willie clung tighter to his mama.

"That's alright," said his mama. "Willie knows, don't you, Son, that it's them that don't get hugging who think it's silly."

Willie looked up into his mama's face, smiling, until he felt a tap on his shoulder. Turning, he saw his daddy smiling down at him. "My turn, Son," he said.

Willie put his arms around his daddy, burying his face in the familiar khaki shirt and feeling once again secure in the warmth of the strong arms around him.

Breakfast tasted better to Willie than it had in many a day. And when it came time to leave for school, Willie gave hugs all around.

Jumping into the big truck, Willie and his daddy stopped by to pick up Jo-Jo. When they arrived at school, Willie reached up and gave his daddy a quick, tight hug. Then he scooted out the door behind Jo-Jo.

"What did you do that for, man?" Jo-Jo said, once they were out of the truck. "Don't you know that's silly?"

Willie gave his friend a shove on the shoulder. Maybe Jo-Jo wouldn't let someone hug him, but he would allow a playful shove now and then. "Go on, now, Jo-Jo," he said. "I think *you're* what's silly."

Jo-Jo ran on ahead. "Help, help!" he
shrieked. "I'm being mugged! Help!"

But Willie didn't mind. He lagged behind,
feeling warm and safe knowing that he was,
after all, the hugging kind.

NEW ROCHELLE PUBLIC LIBRARY

3 1019 15090580 3

J
Barrett, Joyce Durham.
Willie's not the hugging
kind $12.95

OCT 1 0 1991   APR 1 1 1996

FEB - 5 1992
FEB - 1 1993   MAY 2 5 1996
                       JUL 1 6 1996
MAR 1 5 1993
JUL 2 3 1993   FEB 1 1 1997

APR 1 2 1994   MAR - 2 1999

JUN 1 1 1994

JUL 2 8 1994

JAN 2 5 1990

NEW ROCHELLE PUBLIC LIBRARY

Library Plaza

New Rochelle, N.Y.   10801

632-7878

Please telephone for information

on library services and hours